How Our Village Beat the Australians

By

Hugh de Selincourt

British Library Cataloguing-in-Publication Data
A catalogue record for this book is available from
the British Library

Hugh de Selincourt

Hugh de Selincourt was born on 15 June, 1878 and was a prominent English author and Journalist. He is best recalled today for the idyllic tale of village cricket, *The Cricket Match* (1924). Selincourt spent his early education at Dulwich College, moving on to study his degree at Oxford. During the 1910s he worked as a drama critic for *The Star*, an early daily newspaper, and subsequently as a literary critic of the *Observer* which had now become a highly esteemed broadsheet. Selincourt worked for the *Observer* until the outbreak of World War One, however he continued to write book reviews for the newspaper long after his official employment. Selincourt published several comical novels, the first of which was *A Boy's Marriage*, published in 1907 followed by *Young Mischief and Young 'Un* shortly after the war. He spent the interwar years with his wife Janet at their beautiful house 'Sand Pit' in Sussex, and had an open marriage. This was a highly unusual arrangement for 1920s England; to be 'openly open' was a rarity, yet the possible scandal of their relationship did not seem to cause Selincourt nor his wife much hardship. Despite his unconventional home-life, it is the highly traditional and bucolic *The Cricket Match* for which Selincourrt is loved. The book is set in the fictional village of Tillingfold, loosely based on the picturesque hamlets at the bottom of the South Downs where Selincourt spent his childhood. Through a bird's eye perspective, it relates the tales of the various players, rising from their beds – all in different circumstances of life, to be brought together in one common purpose on the village green, only to disperse at nightfall. Selincourt continued writing in the later years of his life, publishing *The Saturday Match* in 1937 and *Gauvinier Takes to Bowls* in 1948. He died at the age of 72 in his home in Sussex, on 20 January 1951. His widow, Janet, died four years later in 1955.

How Our Village Beat the Australians

by Hugh de Selincourt

Here they were – these great Australians with their unbeaten record –
to speak to any of whom by chance even or mistake, in a railway
carriage, would have been an unforgettable honour; here they actually
were in full strength dressed and ready to play us, stepping about on our
own ground – cracking jokes like ordinary men. No wonder our hearts
beat, our eyes bulged, our knees weakened, for after all it is one thing to
talk of having a go at the Australians and quite another to see them in
flesh and blood before you. The thing seemed barely credible. Sam
Bird, who always likes to be careful in his statements – never anxious,
you understand, to commit himself in any way – said to me as I stood
quailing:

'On the whole they're a pretty decent side, I should say; perhaps the
strongest side that has ever appeared on a village ground.'

'Ah, well, on paper!' – I answered, my natural optimism asserting itself immediately. 'And there is always the luck of the game to be taken into account.'

'True for you,' Sam slowly laughed. 'You never know your luck!'

One kept blinking to make quite sure that one's eyes were not playing tricks: but they were not. They were recording plain facts as faithfully as human eyes ever can – which persist, however, in affirming the monotonous rigidity of the earth, against our certain knowledge that it is rushing round the sun in space.

There stood Mr. Armstrong, a little larger even than life, tossing with our Captain. Mr. Armstrong, as always, tossed with great skill, and showed no surprise at winning. He elected to bat without a moment's hesitation, not pausing for a moment to consider the old familiar argument that it is a good thing to know what you have to make before going in to make them. He showed no nervousness of any kind: indeed it was desolating for us to observe the complete confidence that marked the deportment of our visitors. Some of us were cowardly enough to wish that we had left the Australians unchallenged. There was a look too of amusement on the faces of the spectators, who were crowding upon the ground, as though they had left their homes not so much to watch a game of cricket as to see some fun.

Jovial remarks were flung out to us from the safety of the crowded ring – to keep our tails up – to show what we were made of – to remember that no game was lost till it was won. I regret to say they were on the facetious rather than on the encouraging side.

Mr. Collins and Mr. Gregory opened the batting to the bowling of Sid Smith and Mr. Gauvinier. Our side was fairly strong, the same indeed, with two exceptions, as that which defeated Raveley. On paper our side did not look much perhaps; on the field, however, there were great possibilities about it.

Sam Bird, asked to give centre to Mr. Collins, could hardly speak or move; but eventually Mr. Collins obtained as good a block as he has ever obtained in a Test Match.

The curious happenings, which I shall accurately relate as my eyes beheld them, began immediately. For Sid Smith, bewildered by the occasion, bowled as soon as Sam Bird stood back and a little too soon for Mr. Collins, who was not quite ready. Had this occurred in a Test Match, Mr. Collins would undoubtedly have stepped away declining to play the ball, but in this game, as the ball was a full toss, Mr. Collins perhaps opined that he was ready enough to place it out of the ground: for this he gallantly tried to do, but unfortunately he missed the ball altogether and it hit his middle stump.

He looked pardonably and intensely annoyed; Sid and Paul Gauvinier, both real sportsmen, instantly ran up, Sid apologizing and Mr. Gauvinier pointing out that the umpire had omitted to cry 'Play!' (which was true: Sam Bird's lips had indeed moved, but no audible sound had emerged from them). Mr. Gauvinier begged Mrs. Collins to remain where he was, not wishing to take an unfair advantage of any visiting team; in the interests of the game he begged him to stay, and Mr. Collins very obligingly consented to do so. The ball was considered as a no ball, as thought it had never been bowled; and the game was resumed, or perhaps it would be more accurate to say, properly begun.

Sam Bird found his voice and bravely shouted 'Play!' and we all got ready on our toes, taking heart at the mere sight of an Australian wicket broken, however the breaking may have been caused.

Now I am a trained observer and was in a position to see what happened next. Sid bowled his usual medium-to-slow-paced ball on the off stump, and it was a perfect length. Mr. Collins played well forward – to drive it, firmly but not hard, past mid-off: but the ball, instead of striking the bat, rose, as though bouncing on some invisible substance or lifted by some unseen spirit hand, and, describing a near half-circle over the shoulder of his bat, hit the centre of the off stump.

There was a hush of surprise, then a roar of applause. Mr. Collins looked at his bat and looked at the wicket and looked at the pitch. Mr. Collins looked scared. He stooped to pick up the ball; he pinched it, he smelt it, as though in doubt of its being a cricket ball at all; then he uttered a deep-felt ejaculation of regret and withdrew towards our pavilion. He will worry about that ball as long as he worries about anything, and how it came to bowl him. But it was all over, as these tragic and mysterious things always are, in a tiny fraction of a second and no one exists who can really enlighten us as to their exact nature. Even if we happen to be told the truth, we are not able to believe it. We are in fact the merest Horatios and there is far, far more in heaven and earth and also on the cricket field than is dreamed of in our philosophies.

0 – 1 – 0, the score-board read; a familiar, and I may add, under the circumstances, a refreshing sight. Our Secretary, Mr. John McLeod, walked up to Sid Smith, and told him that it was the finest ball he had

ever seen bowled. Sid blushed and believed him and hoped that a member of the English Selection Committee was on the ground, and making a note of his name.

Mr. Armstrong came in next, slow, massive and imperturbable, his enormous belief in his side and himself towering above the little wanton vagaries of Chance.

'Not a bad ball *that*, I should say!' he remarked cheerfully to Sid, twiddling his bat round in his hand, making it look a funny little instrument for such a great man to be using.

Still thrilled by what my eyes had beheld, I rather hoped that nothing unforeseen would happen to him. Moreover 0 – 2 – 0 on the score-board would really be past a joke, would indeed appear almost blasphemous treatment of our august visitors. The Australian Captain was the Australian Captain, and *lèse majesté* is not an empty formula to any but a Communist heart. Perhaps some such thoughts moved Sid, for much to my relief his next ball was a half-volley outside the leg stump which Mr. Armstrong swept gracefully clean out of the ground, narrowly missing a motor that was passing along in the road, its occupants oblivious of who were playing in our field: thus many golden opportunities are missed, as we rush along our modern way at an ever faster pace. Eager small boys found and returned the ball, hopeful of much similar work: but Mr. Armstrong, though his confidence towered above Chance, yet took no liberties with that fickle lady; and played the remaining four balls of the over as any decent first-wicket batsman would have played four good-length balls in his first over.

Tillingfold crossed over, and Mr. Gauvinier started to bowl to Mr. Gregory, and it was clear that Mr. Gregory had the length of the game well in mind, and was determined to waste no time, for the first ball he slashed confidently past cover with such force that it overcame the longish grass and reached the boundary. Two ones followed, confident hard drives which young Mr. Trine flung back from the deep. Mr. Armstrong was backing up with a little more exuberance perhaps than he would have done in a Test Match, suggesting a readiness to play the excellent game of tip-and-run; Mr. Gauvinier bowled a good-length ball on the off stump: Mr. Gregory stepped out and drove it straight back with tremendous force to the bowler, whose hand the ball viciously smacked and then struck the wicket. Unfortunately Mr. Armstrong was a good yard outside his crease and his own umpire was obliged to give him out in response to the yell of appeal that came simultaneously from point, slip, and Mr. Gauvinier, and was taken up immediately from sheer joyous excitement by most of our remaining fieldsmen.

Mr. Armstrong reluctantly withdrew, an illustrious victim of misfortune, and all of us within earshot condoled with him, sincerely, crying out, 'Oh, bad luck, sir, bad luck!'

He smiled and remarked without a quaver in his voice, like the great sportsman that he is: 'It's all in the game, boys; it's all in the game.'

Somehow, we most of us felt guilty, and longed to put him back again at the wicket; but it could not of course be done. Even a great Australian Captain must bow before his fate and the rules of the game.

Mr. Ryder strode in to join Mr. Gregory, and caused considerable amusement to the spectators by hastening to take centre before he realized that he was not to receive the bowling.

Sam Bird started to run from square-leg to the wicket, confident that he and not the famous batsman must be at fault.

He paused half-way and looked wildly round, before returning to his place with his accustomed composure.

Not in the least daunted by the bad start, Mr. Ryder and Mr. Gregory played good free cricket, and it seemed probable that they might make a stand, as the bowling neither of Sid Smith nor of Mr. Gauvinier appeared to trouble them greatly. Twenty was on the score-board; and though Mr. Armstrong and Mr. Collins were out – two useful men to see the back of in any match – signs of uneasiness began to be shown among the Tillingfold team.

Mr. Gregory was lashing good-length balls a little outside the off stump between point and cover; Teddy White was fielding cover and retreated to the boundary by the hedge. Our Secretary, Mr. John McLeod, fearless and short and stout (fearless, that is, of anything but the possible effect of a sudden stoop), was fielding point and came squarer, though the balls seemed generally to have passed him before he was quite aware that they had been hit. He was unaccustomed to the shot and to its pace. Once or twice he had fallen over in a frantic but tardy effort to reach the ball. This had called forth little shouts of laughter from the happy spectators who were not fielding point to Mr. Gregory, and old John McLeod felt that he was somehow being made game of, for a smile was noticeable even upon the courteous face of Mr. Gregory.

I watched this little side-show, as it were, with increasing interest, full of that strained ominous sensation, familiar to us all in dreams, that something startling was about to happen.

Mr. Gregory, with those steel-strong wrists of his, lashed at the ball and hit it a beautiful smack: and I saw Mr. McLeod bound yards to the right with his arm extended, and his arm seemed to stretch out like a piece of elastic; there was another smack, following the first quickly as two reports from a gun. Mr. McLeod spun completely round and sat quietly down with a dazed look upon his face, holding up the caught ball in his right hand, between his fingers and thumb.

Mr. Gregory had started running, thinking his hit was safely away to Teddy White – the howls and yells of joy at the catch stopped him. He stared at Mr. McLeod, bewildered.

'I caught it all right,' our Secretary faltered, and began slowly to rise from his sitting posture. 'It stuck, you know.'

Mr. Gregory continued to stare, first at Mr. McLeod, then out towards Teddie White, in the direction he was sure the ball had travelled, half suspecting, I believe, that Mr. McLeod had played a trick upon him and produced another ball, like a conjurer, from the slack of his breeches.

But Mr. Gregory, though a little dazed with astonishment, was clear-minded enough to perceive that there was no slack to Mr. McLeod's breeches, or, indeed, to any other part of his attire, which fitted him like a glove. The Australian umpire answered his questioning look with becoming promptness:

'Out!' he called, and added to Mr. Gauvinier: 'The most wonderful catch I have ever seen.'

Our Secretary quickly recovered from his momentary surprise as we crowded round him, asking him however he had managed to bring it off. He was so happy that he was on the brink of tears. 'The sort of catch I've often dreamed of making,' he stammered. 'And now I've done it, bless my soul! Now I've done it; and in this game too!'

'We are all inspired once in our lives,' said young Trine, who had come hurrying up from the deep.

'Inspired! Ah, that's the very word,' gasped old John, more breathless than usual. 'Do you know I was that mad to catch it, I felt lifted up and shoved towards it, and as though my arm had got stretched out three times it natural length at least.'

'That's exactly what it looked like, mate,' said Sid Smith in solemn tones. And to the world at large he added: 'This is what comes of playing cricket on a Sunday!' a remark which it baffled me to understand, though local people are often superstitious. Old John McLeod, I thought, looked hurt. But the happy cluster round our honest Secretary broke up as Mr. Andrews strode to the wicket, and the catch, like other great events in human existence, became a thing of the past; a thing to be recounted to grand-children by every person who had seen it; a thing of history; a thing, moreover, so rarely wonderful in itself that it could not possibly be embellished in the telling.

24 – 3 – 11. Tillingford were not doing so badly. It was clear that they were no longer content to make an exhibition of themselves for the country's sake; they were all out now to make a game of it; forgetting in their enthusiasm and excitement that any batsman on the other side might be considered good enough for at least a hundred. If fat old John McLeod could at a pinch hold a catch like that, hang it all! why shouldn't anyone? Thus ran the tenor of their thought.

'Does he often do that?' Mr. Andrews asked our stumper pleasantly, as he made his block, smiling.

'Oh, well! Not very often, now,' our stumper bashfully replied.

Sid Smith was now bowling with more than his usual unconcern, as though he were at length convinced that he could but do his best and that the outcome of his effort lay in other hands than his. There was something impersonal and aloof about his attitude, and his attitude was perhaps a wise one under the circumstances, though in an ordinary game it might have robbed his bowling of sting and intention. But this, it will be noted, was not an ordinary game.

Of course in cricket, the game being played with a moving ball (sometimes a very swiftly moving ball), things happen so quickly and are over so soon that no one can be quite sure precisely what did happen to any given ball. Thus it is we hear even from experts such divergent accounts of the same stroke. The game, indeed, is wrapped in a cloud of mystery which can never be pierced. Herein lies its fascination. The player feels himself in touch with some hidden power, when, for example, leaping out to his full length the bowler takes and holds a flying ball he can barely see. It is not done by taking thought. The man who has ever held a hot return from his own bowling feels that it has somehow been done for him, and feels grateful; the man who has unaccountably missed a sitter at mid-off, which ninety-nine times out of a hundred he would have held, feels that he has been the victim of a spiteful trick.

On the cricket field we are in touch with powers to which, though we may not be in a position to name and label them, as in this mechanical age we like to name and label everything, it is as well to be respectful. It was natural that in such a game as this these powers should be in special evidence, and it was natural that such a simple unsophisticated soul as Sid Smith should be specially open to their influence. There was something comic, no doubt, in the dogged perseverance of his bowling, but there was also something very touching in its faithfulness and simplicity.

Now some of us read with surprise that Jack Hobbs, after playing the Australian bowling for a whole day, was bowled on the opening of the second day by a full toss from Mr. Mailey. We had learned at our preparatory schools that a full toss was a good ball to smite. Jack Hobbs himself, however, in the interesting account of the tour which he contributed to a daily newspaper, described himself as being quite content to be out to such a ball, which, we were told, was deceptive in pace, swerved in its flight, hung in the air, and beat him all ends up before bowling him.

I must own to having been sceptical about this until with my own eyes I saw the ball with which Sid Smith disturbed the wicket of Mr. Ryder. It, too, was a full toss, a slow full toss, which I thought, and Mr. Ryder obviously thought, must reach him knee-high wide of the wicket on the leg side. But, halfway in its flight, just after Mr. Ryder had turned, his mind, in that fraction of a second during which a batsman unconsciously decides to act, made up, his strength summoned – half-way in its flight, I say, the ball miraculously seemed to pause and swerve inwards. Mr. Ryder, observing this, made a superb effort to change his mind, only possible to such a fine batsman as he is, but in spite of his almost superhuman quickness of eye and wrist, he was too late; he over-balanced as the ball swerved gently past him and on to the middle stump and neatly saved himself from a fall by the help of his bat. A clumsier man would certainly have fallen.

Mr. Macartney came in next, looking perceptibly worried at the way things were going. A village wicket might be accountable for a great deal, but no wicket could be blamed for disaster caused by a full toss.

There was a business-like look about him, the air of one who without being the least downhearted or inclined to sit upon the splice, was yet determined to take no foolish risks. It was evident that he considered the previous batsmen had been victims either of gross ill-luck, like Mr. Armstrong, or of their own folly.

Three runs were made without any untoward incident. Mr. Macartney and his partner seemed to be wondering how four good wickets could have fallen; their voices as they called, to run or not to run, had that settled confidence of men who are ready to go quietly on till their Captain sees fit to declare. But this was not to be.

Mr. Macartney drove Mr. Gauvinier past mid-off into the deep to young Mr. Trine. As the batsmen passed, Mr. Andrews said, 'There's another,' and there seemed no doubt whatever that there was ample time for a second run.

Mr. Trine was fielding alertly and well – he saw their intention to take a second run: at full speed he picked the ball up and flung it in with such force and accuracy that the middle stump was knocked clean out of the ground. It was fortunate the stump was not broken, as there might have been considerable difficulty in obtaining another: and we never like to ask any side to finish the game with incomplete kit. Mr. Andrews, noticing the amazing velocity of the throw, quickened his pace, but being a good yard outside the crease was forced to retire.

You could not call the piece of work that dismissed him with any justice a fluke. True, Mr. Trine did not usually throw with such pace and accuracy: indeed, he seemed spirited to the ball even as the ball was spirited to the wicket; but most men rise to an occasion once at least in their lives; and that was the occasion on which Mr. Trine rose; nor could he have chosen a better. It is unlikely that he will ever forget that piece of fielding; it is certain that he will never repeat it.

Tillingfold continued to do quite nicely; five wickets were now down for thirty-three. Of course, the Australian tail might wag, though tails rarely did on our own ground, for long.

Now our Captain, Mr. Gauvinier, is always mad to win; some people say that he is over-anxious, too keen. He may possibly be; but I think he was wise to remind the side that they had to face some pretty decent bowling. He did not overdo it, as he would have done had he gone on to remind us that on several well-authenticated occasions all ten wickets of a side had fallen without a run being scored. We had all read these lamentable records at the end of Mr. Somerset's score-book; and they had long been present somewhere at the back of most of our minds as a painful possibility, though no one, I am glad to say, had had the indecency to put the horrid thought into words.

Mr. Mailey came in quite unabashed by the figures on the score-board. By the way he took centre you felt he was going to make things hum. He did. He leaped out at Mr. Gauvinier's first ball and hit it full and tremendously hard. I thought it must have gone well into the next field. I was astonished accordingly to hear Mr. Gauvinier call out, in a loud commanding voice, 'Mine!' I looked up, and there the ball was soaring higher and higher; so high indeed that Mr. Mailey and Mr. Macartney easily ran two before the ball descended into Mr. Gauvinier's safe hands, about a yard and a half behind the umpire. The way in which Mr. Gauvinier avoided treading on the wicket was extremely clever.

Tillingfold have always been proud of their fielding. They had certainly never shown to better advantage. 'The feller deserves to be out,' growled Mr. Macartney, 'swiping at his first ball in that silly fashion.'

Mr. Mailey walked jauntily out, laughing to himself, pretending bravely, as many another good cricketer has pretended on that sad walk to the pavilion after failing to score, that after all it didn't so very much matter.

Small boys were pacing up and down before the pavilion, peering in to catch a glimpse of Mr. Armstrong's face; but the features of such a man are under perfect control, and they learned nothing of what was passing behind the cheerful mask within the great man's mind. All captains should strive to acquire this imperturbability of feature, as a rattled skipper is apt to mean a disjointed side. Mr. Armstrong's bearing was indeed a lesson to us all. His plan had no doubt been to make a couple of hundred or so for the loss of one or perhaps two wickets, to take tea and then skittle us twice out for twenty or perhaps thirty. But the gods who preside over cricket had decided otherwise; the unforeseen had happened; and six good wickets were down for thirty-three. Nothing can alter a fact of this kind: each fallen wicket helped to form, like boulders, a horrid little cairn of incontrovertible fact.

The remaining Australian batsmen gave us little trouble, and nobody expected that they would. As Sid Smith wisely remarked: 'We had 'em on the run,' and a side in that condition, as everyone knows, can do nothing right. Our men, on the other hand, did nothing whatever wrong. Every semblance of a catch was held, and some, indeed, that hardly bore any ordinary resemblance to a catch. That, for instance, with which young Mr. Trine dismissed Mr. McDonald was quite miraculous. The ball, travelling at the deadly breast-high level of a furious drive, seemed well out of reach; but Mr. Trine, speeding over the rough ground with the effortless ease of a man moving like a porpoise through water in his dreams, did reach it and he held it superbly in his outstretched hand. Wonderful as the catch was, he never looked like missing it.

The Australian innings closed at thirty-nine – a trebly unlucky number.

There was time for thirty-five minutes' batting before the tea interval at five. It created a very favourable impression that quite a number of the Australian team walked with a hand on the roller, while we rolled the wicket.

Some of us were wondering whether Mr. Armstrong, in view of important matches that were to be played during the week, would think it wiser to rest his fast bowlers, in spite of the fact that the wicket would certainly suit them; and distrustful eyes were turned on certain unobtrusive plaintains that, do what we would, continued to disfigure the square.

As the roller was shoved up by the hedge I noticed an Eastern gentleman who was staying in the village and was rumoured to be a Tibetan monk of very high grade, left standing alone. He approached each wicket and inspected the stumps, stroking each one gently between his finger and thumb, as though to find out the quality of the material of which they were made. Sam Bird told me that, before the game began, he had asked to be allowed to handle the ball, and Sam had allowed him to do so.

'Ah, how ingenious men are!' he had remarked, as he politely handed the ball back to Sam.

Sam Bird likes to do everything properly. He realized that our visitors were accustomed to play on county grounds where a bell is rung to warn spectators off the ground and to prepare the team for taking the field. There is no bell on our ground; the umpires stroll out and we follow at our leisure; so thoughtful Sam, afraid that the Australians might be put off their game by the absence of the tintinnabulation to which their ears were accustomed, had brought a small bell and this he produced from his trouser pocket and shook violently for some moments, standing discreetly, being a shy man, behind the small scoring-box. Then, with some difficulty replacing the bell in his trouser pocket, he joined his colleague and proceeded with a solemn shy smile upon his broad face to the wicket, followed by the Australian team in a laughing, compact body.

Our Secretary, dear old John McLeod, who was going in first and always took first ball, turned a little pale when he saw that Mr. Armstrong, suitably impressed by Tillingford's magnificent fielding, was setting his field for a fast bowler.

'Oh dear!' he said. 'Bless my soul, now. Oh, well. One ball. How I should dearly love to play a ball or two.'

'You just stop there till tea,' said Mr. Gauvinier pleasantly, patting him on the back. 'And we shall be all right.'

'It's no good waiting,' said Mr. Bois, a preparatory schoolmaster who lived in the village and had played much really good cricket. 'Come on. The sound old rules hold good, you know. Keep your eye on the ball and use a nice straight bat.'

They made their brave way to the wicket.

Dear old John McLeod must have felt not more than about three inches high, as all alone he faced Mr. McDonald and the ten Australian fieldsmen, placed by a master mind on the exact spot towards which, if he did happen to stroke the ball, the ball must certainly fly. Mr. McDonald came thundering along his terrific run to the wicket, a giant with a cannon ball which a man feeling like a midget was to receive with a bat that felt like half a wax match in the midget's grasp. The odds were disproportionate. But our Secretary, all honour to him, gripped the handle of his bat, glued his eye on something he took to be the ball and played the ball.

Its impact on the centre of his bat gave Mr. McLeod such confidence that he grew from a mere midget of a few inches to almost half his full stature as a man. True, he dwindled a little as Mr. McDonald walked leisurely into the outfield preparatory to delivering his next ball, but during the course of the five seconds' sprint to the wicket he had time to grow once more, and once more the ball met the bat though sooner than Mr. McLeod had expected. This second stroke drew a round of applause from the spectators, confident now that the batsman had taken the measure of the bowling. The next ball, however, missed the bat. Mr. Oldfield, confident that it must hit the wicket, missed it also and it sped to the boundary for four runs.

Thus Tillingfold's worst fears of dismissal without scoring were allayed. A jubilant smile spread slowly over many of the faces of the team in the pavilion.

'Oh Lord,' Horace Cairie muttered, 'if we could only beat them!' And he kept doing the sum six sixes are thirty-six and a bye or a leg-bye could sometimes score six.

The next ball also missed the bat, and missed the wicket. I was standing straight behind the stumps and I was as surprised as Mr. Oldfield and Mr. McDonald at Mr. McLeod's escape. I could have sworn that the top of the wicket faced for that fraction of a second when the ball should have struck it. But there stood the wicket, bails on, unbroken. Mr. Oldfield walked up to the stumps, put both his gloved hands on them, and pressed them, as wicket-keepers sometimes do, backwards and forwards, as though to assure himself that there was no deception.

Mr. McDonald may be pardoned for stamping with vexation when the same thing happened to all the remaining balls of his over except the last, which Mr. McLeod steered with a quick flick of his wrist through a small crowd of slips bang against the pavilion for four.

I did not know that Mr. McLeod kept such a shot in his locker. But it has been well said that good bowling evokes latent powers from a batsman. Mr. Bois was never tired of impressing this upon us when urging us, as he frequently did, to make a point of playing better sides. It was chiefly through his advocacy, as the son of a millionaire who had great influence in Melbourne attended his school, that the game had been arranged.

Mr. Bois played with his usual unruffled composure, though his wicket too was often missed by a miracle. Once the wicket was perceptibly hit and perceptibly trembled, but the bails remained stolidly in their place; and there was nothing wrong with the set of the wicket or with the bails, because Mr. Oldfield tapped the stumps lightly with his finger and the bails dropped lightly off. Their umpire, too, came forward and shook the wicket as Mr. Oldfield had done.

It must have been thankless work for their bowlers, for I suppose our first-wicket batsmen might perhaps be considered mere rabbits to bowlers of their class, and to keep shaving the stumps of a rabbit is distressing to any bowler. Then these men, it must be remembered, had the honour of a great Commonwealth to sustain; and to them therefore these elusive wickets must have been doubly, nay, trebly trying. They clutched their heads, they stamped their feet, they jerked their arms down as though punching imaginary heads: and ever the confidence of the two batsmen became more bland and smiling, as well it may have done. The way the Australian bowlers stuck to their thankless task commanded our admiration and roused our unstinted applause.

Runs, however, did not come so fast as in the first over. Mr. Oldfield was alert behind the stumps; the small crowd of slips were on their toes: the fielding, though not miraculous, was very good. Ten, however, crept up on the board, and our batsmen would certainly have remained together until the tea interval, had not Mr. Bois, in playing back to Mr. McDonald, unfortunately struck his wicket with his bat. The one blemish to his style is that he is apt to cramp his freedom of movement by making his block unnecessarily far back from the front crease.

11 – 1 – 5 the score-board read, and though Tillingfold as a team would have liked to have knocked off the thirty-nine runs without loss, the start could not be described as other than quite satisfactory. Mr. Bois, however, was extremely annoyed. He was quite at home, he said, and could have stayed there for hours, had it not been for his execrable luck.

Young Mr. Trine, who came in next, noticing that Mr. Oldfield was standing well back and that there was no fieldsman in the deep, determined to have a go. As Mr. McDonald was taking his sprint to the wicket he shambled along out of his ground to meet him and letting madly fly, drove him well out of the ground. A few small boys remained husky for the remainder of the day after the prolonged yell which the fine daring of this hit elicited.

He tried to repeat this manœuvre on the last ball of the over, but he started too soon and got too far out of his ground, so that Mr. McDonald and Mr. Oldfield foresaw his intention and acting like one man, Mr. McDonald bowled a slow high full toss over Mr. Trine's head into the hands of Mr. Oldfield who, still on the run, stumped him – a brilliant piece of concerted work between bowler and wicket-keeper.

'Ah!' said Sid Smith sagely, wagging his head. 'You dussn't take no liberties with such as they.'

During tea, as is usually the case, the strain of the contest was relaxed. The Tillingfold team, especially those who had not yet faced the fast bowlers, seemed to enjoy the honour of eating with their distinguished visitors even more than the honour of playing cricket with them.

Crowds paraded in front of the pavilion, glancing in, as to many it was quite as thrilling to know how the Australians drank their tea and ate their cake and bread and butter as to watch them bat and bowl. Our visitors showed no surprise at this interest, since the trait is common to the inhabitants of both continents, and were no more put off their food by spectators than they were put off their game by them.

Many of the Tillingfold team, however, unused to the glare of publicity, were painfully affected and, much to the distress of their thoughtful captain, ate and drank next to nothing – comparatively speaking – though the caterer had provided a special tea and had raised the price from ninepence to one shilling.

Punctual to the moment Sam Bird, a cake in his mouth, a pastry in his hand (sensible fellow, his bashfulness had limits), tore himself from the table and producing the little bell from his trouser pocket, rang it vigorously, faithful to duty and unheeding the rude remarks of small boys who gathered eagerly about him as he leaned against the small scoring-box.

The umpires went out together. Mr. Armstrong led his men once more into the field, with a look at the score-board which read 17 – 2 – 6. The great game was resumed, Mr. Fanshawe joining our Secretary at the wicket.

Mr. Fanshawe takes his cricket very seriously. He is a religious bat, treating a half-volley or a long hop on the leg with reverence. He was in fact the ideal man to bat first in a Test Match where time is no consideration: during the first week he would have played himself steadily in, and towards the end of the second week he would have begun to make runs, and no one knows how freely he might not have scored as the innings proceeded. But in the Tillingfold games, having always felt hurried, he had never really done himself justice – a born Test Match player in village cricket: another square peg in a round hole. Alas! Life abounds with them.

No doubt Mr. McDonald and Mr. Gregory hoped that, after being refreshed with a cup of tea and bite of bread and butter, they would be able to hit the wickets; but though they bowled uncommonly well and frequently beat the batsmen the wickets remained intact, as they had done before tea.

In the first half-hour two leg-byes were scored off their bowling; and Mr. Armstrong, feeling that his fast bowlers were expensive and fatiguing themselves to no good purpose, made a double change, going on himself with Mr. Mailey.

Mr. McLeod, never a forcing bat, became infected with Mr. Fanshawe's religious caution, and the atmosphere was so charged with reverence that a run off the bat began to appear like a profanity.

The crowd, at first respectful at the steady resistance to the Australian attack, at last grew restive and disrespectful. Indeed they showed signs of barracking, thinking possibly that it was a mistake to be playing for a draw with twenty-one runs to make to win and more than an hour's time to make them in. They barracked to deaf ears: Mr. McLeod and Mr. Fanshawe, even had their tenacity of purpose allowed them to hear a sound were not light-natured enough to be distracted by popular opinion, much as each loved his fellow man off the cricket ground. Mr. Mailey tried every conceivable wile to tempt Mr. Fanshawe to hit; but Mr. Fanshawe was not to be tempted. Around both batsmen all the fieldsmen clustered in indescribable positions, sillier than silly. But both batsmen were well content to smother every ball that might under ordinary circumstances have hit the wicket, and let all others severely alone. In the second half-hour after tea, one more leg-bye had been scored. Twenty stood on the score-board – it looked with a quarter of an hour to go as though the match must end in a draw.

But cricket is a game of infinite uncertainty. At last, in desperation, Mr. Andrews, unable to bear it any longer, literally flung himself at Mr. Fanshawe's bat just as the ball struck it, and caught him well within the crease. It looked more like a tackle at Rugby football than a catch at cricket; and Mr. Fanshawe, rather bewildered, appealed against it, but he appealed in vain. The catch was unusual and unorthodox, but he was indubitably out.

Teddie White came in next. Australians or no Australians he came in, as he always came in, at a half-trot, shouldering his bat, to get to business with as little delay as possible. He disliked formalities, leaving them gladly to what he called 'the rank and stink.'

Mr. Armstrong, caught no doubt after this slow hour in the general assumption that runs were a profanity, or perhaps thinking that the Tillingfold captain had given his men instructions to play for a draw neglected to replace his field: they were only a little less on the cluster round Teddie White than they had been round Mr. Fanshawe.

Teddie White did not go in for niceties; he didn't bother about the field; it didn't matter to him where they happened to be placed; his one aim in batting was to put the ball out of their reach, out of the ground, much the safest place. But he had a kind heart and noticing that the fieldsmen were crowded rather nearer to him than they usually were, as Mr. Armstrong bowled, he cried out: 'Look out for yourselves then,' as he might have done to careless boys at the village net, and lashed it for four.

There was a roar of applause. But Teddie White was not pleased. It was an ass of a shot – all along the ground – he had not properly got hold of it at all – you could never hit a six like that, the only really safe shot.

Mr. Armstrong much dislikes to be caught napping. He set his master mind to work, sized up his man exactly with one piercing look, and proceeded to dot his men carefully along the leg-side boundary, confident that the next ball would prove this reckless hitter's downfall.

Teddie chafed at the delay, muttering to himself: 'If I be dratted fool enough not to beat it over their Aussie 'eads!'

At length, Mr. Armstrong, satisfied with the exact position of his field, swung in his next delivery with a quiet smile of confidence. Teddie White burst at it in mad fury like an explosion; not a muscle, not a nerve in his body but he used for that frenzied blow – the vein on his forehead even bulged, as he smote the ball whizzing over the pavilion.

'That's one on 'em!' he muttered, crumpling off his little cap and rubbing his thick neck with it. 'Two more of 'em and we wins – with a few to spare.'

Just as some writers, charming gentle fellows to meet, can only become vocal when they are in a thoroughly bad temper with life, so Teddie White could only do himself full justice as a batsman in a mood of concentrated fury, as though it were an outrage that eleven men should band themselves together to do him out of a knock – especially when he never failed to pay his subscription to the club.

The delay in collecting the ball added to his exasperation. Like some sort of inspired fiend he crashed at Mr. Armstrong's next delivery and whanged it over the hedge, over the road and into the garden of a house opposite the ground.

The excitement became delirious. Everyone stood up and shouted and yelled and cheered: men waved their hats, and flung them towards the sky: women waved their scarves and handkerchiefs.

'That's another of 'em,' Teddie White muttered, giving his face and neck another vindictive rub with his little cap.

'Well hit, sir, well hit!' said Mr. Armstrong, the sportsman in him never wavering at the most critical moment of any game.

Teddie White glared. He was not to be conciliated by any honeyed words. He growled to himself, 'Well 'it!' I'll show the blokes well 'it.' But his fury was part of his batting rather than of his nature, and he looked very red and very shy and very happy.

There was a hush in the roaring, a stillness among the fluttering, waving apparel, one of those tense moments that last a lifetime as Mr. Armstrong delivered the last ball of his over. Spectators held their breath and stared: the only sound was the puff-puff of a belated traction engine as it slowly passed the ground. No one noticed anything funny in the way Teddie White's little crumped cap sat balanced upon his square head.

For once in his life Mr. Armstrong was rattled and did not bowl the ball he intended to bowl; the indended half-volley across which Teddie would certainly have hit became a full toss, at which Teddie viciously slashed with all his furious strength; the ball soared a terrific height, higher and higher; the outfielder hopefully watched it, retreating towards the hedge. Then as the clamour of joy rose, it began to fall and fell straight down the smoke-vomiting chimney of the belated traction engine.

But what is this that is happening? Mr. Oldfield excitedly appealing! The Australians flocking round the wicket! Could the game not be ours now after such a hit? We were all in consternation – having kept our eyes fixed on the ball. But Teddie in the fury of his last blow had managed to jolt off his little crumpled cap which had impishly floated on to the wicket and now sat perched there even more comfortably than it had before perched on his own square head.

It appears that Teddie, feeling an instant draught on his bald head, had started to snatch his cap from the stumps. To the eternal honour of the Australians they had persuaded him from this rash act, for had he dislodged the bail in removing his cap before the ball had safely landed down the traction engine's chimney he would of course have been out. As it was, he was still in . . .

How Our Village Beat the Australians

The whole ground rose and flew at him, the air was thick with fluttering scarves, roaring men, yelling boys, waving arms; even the pavilion rose and streamed like a pennon through the air. The Downs themselves swelled to mountains – the houses capered like lambs, as we carried Teddie White, chanting songs of triumph, through the village High Street.

*   *   *   *

And I awoke, alone on the Tillingfold Cricket Ground, with a few toddlers playing about, that lovely Sunday afternoon; and walked smiling home to tea.